Pete
and the
Pandemic

This book is dedicated to our amazing students and all of the other children doing their best to cope with the COVID-19 pandemic.

It was a cold winter day.
Adults got on and off trains, heading home from work, while children raced off their school buses, eager to get home for their afternoon snack.

Pete was excited. Tonight was his mom's night off work, and his family was having dinner at his favorite restaurant.

His mom was a doctor in the Emergency Room and worked a lot. Pete was proud that his mom helped so many people every day, but he missed her when she was at work.

Bellies full, Pete and his family head home.
He and his sister Ashlee washed up for bed, but Pete wasn't tired.
"Hey, Mom, can I play before bed?" Pete asked.
"Sure, honey," Mom said. "But only five minutes."

Pete was playing with his new building blocks when he overheard his parents talking.
"The virus is getting bad in other countries," his mom said. "It's spreading fast, the hospitals are getting too crowded. They don't have enough room for all of the patients".

Pete wondered what his parents were talking about. A few minutes later, Pete's mom came in to kiss him goodnight, but his worried mind made it difficult to sleep that night.

Weeks passed and Pete had forgotten about the virus until one day he noticed his teachers frequently wiping down desks. They also insisted each child use hand sanitizer as they entered the classroom.

Later that day, Pete's friend Cameron pulled him aside.
"My dad told me there's a crazy virus that's spreading
super fast and making people really really sick!" he said.
Cameron looked worried.
"That must be what my mom and dad were talking
about!" Pete thought.

A few days later, Pete and his family were eating
breakfast when the Governor came on the news.
The virus—which he called COVID-19—had
reached the nearby city.
"That's right across the river!" Dad said.

BREAKING NEW

Covid19 is here

That evening, as Pete was working on his St. Patrick's Day project, the phone rang. It was a message from his school.

"Due to COVID-19, school will be closed until further notice".

"School is CLOSED?! Pete thought. This must really be bad. "How will I learn?"

The next day was strange to say the
least. Pete's dad set up a computer at the
kitchen table, and showed Pete how he
would be learning for a while. Pete logged
into a video chat.

He could see his friends and teachers, but it just wasn't the same. He missed the warm hugs from his teacher each morning. He missed playing on the monkey bars with Cameron at recess. "I really hope I can see them soon" Pete thought.

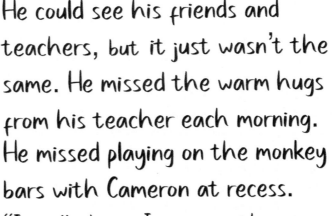

As weeks went by, Pete missed more than just school. He missed his mom. The virus had gotten bad, and she was working extra-long days to help the people who were sick. Pete worried about his mom. He hoped she didn't get sick.

Pete wasn't the only one missing Mom. Ashlee missed her, too. Pete's dad wanted to cheer them up.

He gave each of them a face mask, then said, "C'mon you two. Hop in the car!"

Dad took Pete and Ashlee to the grocery store. When they walked in, Pete's eyes widened. Employees were wiping down carts and baskets. There were arrows on the floor telling customers which way to walk.

And EVERYONE had a face mask on.

Pete, Ashlee, and Dad picked out all the ingredients they needed to make their favorite meal: PIZZA!
At home, they laughed as they tossed the dough in the air and added their favorite toppings. For the first time in a while, the three almost forgot about what was happening in the world.

The weeks dragged on. Pete had a lot of fun with Dad and Ashlee at home, but he still missed his mom and friends. Hearing about the many people getting sick, and families losing people they loved was scary.

It seemed as if there was no end in sight.

"This has been going on for so long. How can we get things back to the way they used to be?" he asked one night at dinner. "It's going to take some time," his mom answered. "But we can help by following the rules that have been given."

"What are the rules?" Pete asked, confused. Pete's mom went on to explain ways to stop the spread of Covid 19.

" Keep a distance from other people. Wear a mask.

Wash and sanitize your hands

Stay home if you feel ill"

As time went on, people followed the rules to keep themselves and others in their community safe. Pete was glad people were getting better, but he was even happier to have more time with his mom.

Pizza making nights were even better with her there!
Life was still very different than it had once been, but
things were getting better.

Pete found the good that had come out of this difficult time, like spending quality time with his family.

Even without school, Pete had learned something.
He realized just how important his family and
friends truly were, and that was something he
would never take for granted.

Made in the USA
Middletown, DE
07 September 2020